The illustrations are for John Whyte

First American Edition. Illustrations Copyright © Errol Le Cain, 1981
All rights reserved

Published in 1981 by The Viking Press, 625 Madison Avenue, New York, N.Y. 10022
Printed in Great Britain
1   2   3   4   5   85   84   83   82   81

Library of Congress Cataloging in Publication Data
Lang, Andrew, 1844–1912.
Aladdin and the wonderful lamp
SUMMARY: Recounts the tale of a poor tailor's son who becomes a wealthy prince
with the help of a magic lamp he finds in an enchanted cave.
[1. Fairy tales   2. Folklore, Arab]   I. Le Cain, Errol.   II. Aladdin.   III. Title
PZ8.L15Al   1981   398.2'2   81–4861
ISBN 0–670–11146–5   AACR2.

Aladdin
and the Wonderful Lamp

retold by

ANDREW LANG

illustrated by

ERROL LE CAIN

THE VIKING PRESS
New York

THERE ONCE lived in Persia a boy called Aladdin. One day when he was playing in the street a stranger asked him his age, and if he was not the son of Mustapha the tailor.

"I am, sir," replied Aladdin, "but he died a long while ago."

At this the stranger fell on his neck and kissed him, saying, "I am your uncle and I knew you from your likeness to my brother. Go to your mother and tell her I am coming."

Aladdin ran home and told his mother of his newly found uncle.

"Indeed, child," she said, "your father had a brother, but I always thought he was dead."

However, she prepared supper and bade Aladdin seek his uncle, who came laden with wine and fruit. He told Aladdin's mother not to be surprised at not having seen him before, as for forty years he had been out of the country.

Next day he led Aladdin a long way outside the city gates until they came to two mountains divided by a narrow valley. "We will go no farther," he said. "I will show you something wonderful. Gather up sticks while I kindle a fire."

When the fire was lit, he threw on it a powder he had with him, at the same time saying some strange words. The earth trembled a little and opened in front of them, disclosing a square flat stone with a brass ring in the middle to raise it by. Aladdin tried to run away, but his uncle caught him and gave him a blow that knocked him down.

"What have I done, Uncle?" he said piteously.

Whereupon his uncle said more kindly, "Fear nothing, but obey me. Beneath this stone lies a treasure that is to be yours, and no one else may touch it, so you must do exactly as I tell you."

At the word "treasure", Aladdin forgot his fears and grasped the ring as he was told. The stone came up quite easily, and some steps appeared.

"Go down," said his uncle. "At the foot of those steps you will find an open door leading into three large halls. Tuck up your robe and go through them without touching anything, or you will die instantly. These halls lead into a garden of fine fruit trees. Walk on till you come to a niche in a terrace where stands a lighted lamp. Pour out the oil it contains and bring it to me." He drew a ring from his finger and gave it to Aladdin, bidding him prosper.

Aladdin found everything as his uncle had said, gathered some fruit off the trees and, having got the lamp, arrived at the mouth of the cave.

His uncle cried out in a great hurry, "Make haste and give me the lamp." This Aladdin refused to do until he was out of the cave. His uncle flew into a terrible rage and, throwing some more powder on the fire, he said something, and the stone rolled back into its place.

This man had only pretended to be Aladdin's uncle. He was really a cunning magician who had read in his magic books of a wonderful lamp that would make him the most powerful man in the world. Though he alone knew where to find it, he could receive it only from the hand of Aladdin. Now, since he could not force the boy to give him the lamp, he returned to Africa, whence he had come.

Aladdin remained in the dark, crying and lamenting. At last he clasped his hands in prayer, and in so doing rubbed the ring, which the magician had forgotten to take from him.

Immediately a genie rose out of the earth, saying, "What wouldst thou with me? I am the slave of the ring and will obey thee in all things."

Aladdin fearlessly replied, "Deliver me from this place," whereupon the earth opened, and he found himself outside. When he came home he told his mother what had passed, and showed her the lamp and the fruits he had gathered in the garden, which were in reality precious stones. He then asked for some food.

"Alas, child," she said, "I have nothing in the house, but I have spun a little cotton and will go and sell it."

Aladdin bade her keep her cotton, for he would sell the lamp instead. As it was very dirty she began to rub it, that it might fetch a higher price. Instantly a genie appeared and asked what she would have.

She fainted away, but Aladdin, snatching the lamp, said boldly, "Fetch me something to eat!"

The genie returned with a golden bowl, twelve gold plates containing rich meats, two gold cups, and a bottle of wine.

Aladdin's mother, when she came to herself, said, "Whence comes this splendid feast?"

"Ask not, but eat," replied Aladdin.

So they sat at breakfast till it was dinner time, and Aladdin told his mother about the lamp. When they had eaten all the genie had brought, Aladdin sold one of the gold plates, and so on till none were left. He then summoned the genie, who gave him another set of plates, and thus they lived for some years.

One day Aladdin heard an order from the sultan proclaiming that everyone was to stay at home and close the shutters while the princess, his daughter, went to and from the bath. Aladdin was seized by a desire to see her face, which was very difficult as she always went veiled. He hid himself behind the door of the bath and peeped through a chink.

The princess lifted her veil as she went in, and looked so beautiful that Aladdin fell in love with her at first sight. He went home and told his mother that he loved the princess so deeply he could not live without her and meant to ask her father for her hand in marriage. His mother, on hearing this, burst out laughing, but Aladdin at last prevailed upon her to go before the sultan and carry his request.

She fetched a napkin and laid in it the magic fruits from the enchanted garden, which sparkled and shone like the most beautiful jewels. The grand vizier and the lords of council had just gone into the palace hall as she arrived, so she went up to the foot of the throne and remained kneeling until the sultan said to her, "Rise, good woman, and tell me what you want."

She hesitated, so the sultan bade her speak freely, promising to forgive her beforehand for anything she might say. She then told him of her son's violent love for the princess.

"I prayed him to forget her," she said, "but in vain; he threatened to do some desperate deed if I refused to go and ask Your Majesty for the hand of the princess. Now I pray you to forgive not me alone but my son Aladdin."

The sultan asked her kindly what she had in the napkin, whereupon she unfolded the jewels and presented them.

He was thunderstruck, and turning to the vizier, said, "What sayest thou? Ought I not to bestow the princess on one who values her at such a price?"

The vizier, who wanted her for his own son, begged the sultan to withhold her for three months, in the course of which he hoped his son would contrive to make a richer present. The sultan granted this and told Aladdin's mother that, though he consented to the marriage, she must not appear before him again for three months.

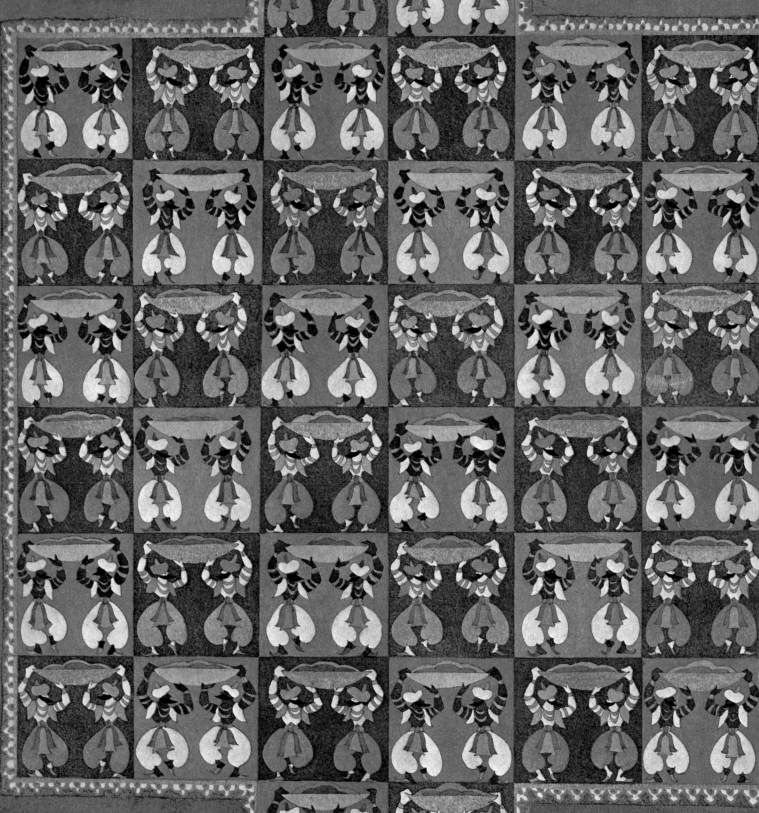

Aladdin waited patiently for nearly three months, but then his mother, going into the city to buy oil, found everyone rejoicing and asked what was going on.

"Do you not know," was the answer, "that the son of the grand vizier is to marry the sultan's daughter tomorrow?"

Breathless, Aladdin's mother ran and told him, and he sent her to remind the sultan of his promise.

The sultan said to her, "Good woman, your son must first send me forty basins of gold brimful of jewels, carried by forty black slaves and as many white ones, splendidly dressed. Tell him that I await his answer."

The mother of Aladdin bowed low and went home, thinking all was lost. She gave Aladdin the message, adding, "He may wait long enough for your answer!"

"Not so long, Mother, as you think," her son replied. "I would do a great deal more than that for the princess." He summoned the genie, and in a few moments the eighty slaves arrived and filled up the small house and garden.

Aladdin made them set out to the palace, followed by his mother, who presented them to the sultan.

He hesitated no longer, but said, "Good woman, return and tell your son that I wait for him with open arms."

She lost no time in telling Aladdin, bidding him make haste, but Aladdin first called the genie.

"I want a scented bath," he said, "richly embroidered clothes, a horse surpassing the sultan's, and fourteen slaves to attend me. Besides this I desire six slaves, beautifully dressed, to wait on my mother; and lastly, ten thousand pieces of gold in fourteen basins."

No sooner said than done. Aladdin mounted his horse and passed through the streets, the slaves strewing gold as they went.

When the sultan saw him, he came down from his throne, embraced him, and led him into a hall where a feast was spread, intending to marry him to the princess that very day. But Aladdin refused, saying, "I must build a palace fit for her," and took his leave.

Once home, he said to the genie, "Build me a palace of the finest marble, set with precious stones. In the middle you shall build me a large hall, each side having six windows. There must be stables and horses and grooms and slaves. Go and see about it!"

The palace was finished the next day, and the genie carried Aladdin there and showed him all his orders faithfully carried out, even to the laying of a velvet carpet from his palace to the sultan's. Aladdin's mother then dressed herself carefully and walked to the palace with her slaves. The sultan sent musicians with trumpets and cymbals to meet them, and the air resounded with music and cheers.

At night the princess said goodbye to her father and set out on the carpet for Aladdin's palace, with his mother at her side, and followed by the hundred slaves. After the wedding had taken place, Aladdin led her into the hall, where a feast was spread, and she supped with him, after which they danced till midnight.

They lived in peace and contentment for several years, but far away in Africa the magician remembered Aladdin and by his magic arts discovered that instead of perishing in the cave he had escaped and had married a princess, with whom he was living in great honour and wealth. He knew that the poor tailor's son could have accomplished this only by means of the lamp, and he travelled day and night till he reached the capital of Persia. As he passed through the town he heard people talking everywhere about a marvellous palace.

"Forgive my ignorance," he said. "What is this palace you speak of?"

"Have you not heard of Prince Aladdin's palace," was the reply, "the greatest wonder of the world? I will direct you if you have a mind to see it."

When he saw the palace, the magician knew that it had been raised by the genie of the lamp. He bought a dozen copper lamps, put them into a basket, and went to the palace, crying, "New lamps for old!", followed by a jeering crowd.

The princess, sitting in the hall of four and twenty windows, sent a slave to find out what the noise was about. The slave came back laughing, so the princess scolded her.

"Madam," replied the slave, "who can help laughing to see an old fool offering to exchange fine new lamps for old ones?"

Another slave, hearing this, said, "There is an old one on the cornice there that he can have."

Now this was the magic lamp, which Aladdin had left there when he went hunting. The princess, not knowing its value, laughingly bade the slave take it and make the exchange. She went and said to the magician, "Give me a new lamp for this."

He snatched it and bade the slave take her choice, amid the jeers of the crowd. Then he went out of the city gates to a lonely place, where he remained till nightfall, when he pulled out the lamp and rubbed it. The genie appeared and at the magician's command carried him, together with the palace and the princess in it, to Africa.

Next morning the sultan looked out of the window towards Aladdin's palace and rubbed his eyes, for it was gone. He sent thirty men on horseback to fetch Aladdin in chains. They met him riding home, bound him, and forced him to go with them on foot.

He was brought before the sultan, and begged to know what he had done.

"False wretch," said the sultan, "come hither," and showed him from the window the place where his palace had stood. Aladdin was so amazed that he could not say a word.

"Where are the palace and my daughter?" demanded the sultan. "For the first I am not so deeply concerned, but my daughter I must have and you must find her or lose your head."

Aladdin begged for forty days in which to find her, promising, if he failed, to return and suffer death at the sultan's pleasure. His prayer was granted and he went forth sadly from the sultan's presence. For three days he wandered about like a madman, asking everyone what had become of his palace, but they only laughed and pitied him.

He came to the banks of a river and knelt down to say his prayers before throwing himself in. In so doing he rubbed the magic ring he still wore. The genie he had seen in the cave appeared and asked his will.

"Save my life, genie," said Aladdin, "and bring my palace back."

"That is not in my power," said the genie. "I am only the slave of the ring; you must ask the slave of the lamp."

"Even so," said Aladdin, "but thou canst take me to the palace, and set me down under my dear wife's window." He at once found himself in Africa, under the window of the princess, where he fell asleep from sheer weariness.

Next morning she looked out and saw him. She called to him to come to her, and great was their joy at seeing each other again.

After he had kissed her Aladdin said, "I beg of you, Princess, before we speak of anything else, for your own sake and mine, tell me what has become of an old lamp I left on the cornice in the hall of four and twenty windows, when I went hunting."

"Alas," she said, "I am the innocent cause of our sorrows," and told him of the exchange of the lamp.

"Now I know," cried Aladdin, "that we have to thank the magician for this. Where is the lamp?"

"He carries it about with him," said the princess. "I know, for he pulled it out of his robe to show me. He wishes me to break my faith with you and marry him, saying that you were beheaded by my father's command."

Aladdin comforted her and went into the nearest town, where he bought a certain powder. Then he returned to the princess, who let him in by a little side door.

"Put on your most beautiful dress," he said to her, "and receive the magician with smiles, leading him to believe that you have forgotten me. Invite him to sup with you and say you wish to taste the wine of this country. He will go for some and I will tell you what to do while he is gone."

She listened carefully to Aladdin, and, when he left her, arrayed herself gaily for the first time since she left Persia. Then she received the magician, saying, "I have made up my mind that Aladdin is dead and that all my tears will not bring him back to me, so I am resolved to mourn no more and therefore invite you to sup with me. But I am tired of the wines of Persia and would fain taste those of Africa."

The magician flew to his cellar and the princess put the powder Aladdin had given her in her cup. When he returned she asked him to drink her health in the wine of Africa, handing him her cup in exchange for his as a sign that she was reconciled to him. She set her cup to her lips while he drained his to the dregs and fell back in a deep sleep.

The princess then opened the door to Aladdin, who took the lamp from the sleeping magician and summoned the genie. He bade him carry the magician outside and then transport the palace and all in it back to Persia. This was done, and the princess felt only two slight shocks and could hardly believe she was at home again.

The sultan, who was sitting in his closet mourning for his lost daughter, happened to look up and rubbed his eyes, for there stood the palace as before! He hastened thither, and Aladdin received him in the hall of the four and twenty windows, with the princess at his side.

After this Aladdin and his wife lived in peace. He succeeded the sultan when he died, and reigned for many years, leaving behind him a long line of kings.